Come and meet...

The Characters of Christmas

Colouring Book

Ruth Hearson

A very long time ago, God's

ProPhets

told everyone that one day,
Jesus would be born.

An angel spoke to

Joseph

in a dream. He told him
to take good care of
Mary and her baby.

Jesus,

God's Son.

The Saviour of our world.

In the stable,

Mary

wrapped baby Jesus
in blankets and placed
Him in a manger.

"Good news!" said the

angel,

"The Messiah has been born today in Bethlehem."

When the

shepherds

had seen baby Jesus,
they were so excited they
told everyone about Him.

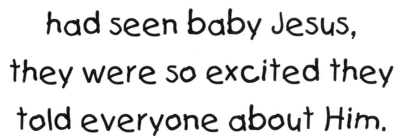

When

heard about Jesus,
he was not happy.
He didn't like God at all!

WISE MEN

followed the shiniest star
in the sky and it took
them all the way to Jesus.

The characters of Christmas
are all part of God's big story.

When **you** love and follow Jesus, you can be part of the story too.

Published by 10Publishing, a division of 10ofThose Limited.
ISBN 978-1-910587-78-2

Typeset by: Diane Warnes
Printed in China

10Publishing, a division of 10ofthose.com
Unit C, Tomlinson Road, Leyland, Lancashire, PR25 2DY England
Email: info@10ofthose.com
Website: www.10ofthose.com